Library of Congress Cataloging In Publication Data
Mellen, Frank If only I could whistle loudly /
prose by Frank Mellen, illustrations by Ray Dirgo
Bridgeport, CT: Greene Bark Press, 1966. [40] P.: ill.; cm.
    Summary: An uplifting circus book which
holds us all enthralled while feats of daring
and splendor are performed. It is only as the circus
comes to a close that we, the readers, realize that life
is the real circus.
II. Title 1. Circus—Fiction.
I. Dirgo, Ray. illustrator 96-76389
ISBN: 1-880851-23-7

"If only I could whistle loudly!"

written by

FRANK MELLEN

illustrated by

RAY DIRGO

Greene Bark Press

To the Little Dirgos

Jocelyn
Emily
Tom
Brian
Victor II

and

Frank Mellen's granddaughter:

Chloe

The

melting snow
with
its ear
to the ground

hears
the circus
coming
down
the

road.

ARRIVING

under
starry sky

the circus train
brushed
sawdust

from
its sleepy

eye.

circus
sleeps
with its dream

tucked
in
a

somersault.

"ZZZZZZZZZZZZ

snored
the zebra

dreaming

of

kicking

a human

in the pants

A circus poster morning

with impossible performance

was
hung
in the sky
to

see.

My

pup
buries bones
on the lot
&
can't
find them
in
the
morning.

A rabbit
ate the flower
I watered
every
day.

The
WIND
blows through town

when
a circus
is
in
it.

NATURE

performed
circus
of the clouds
above

me.

RUUUUUUUUUM BLING

thunder:...
a drum roll
snapping attention
to the
sword
lightning bolt

from
above

earth swallows

like
a side show
trouper
on the

road.

heard
the string puppet
of rain

dance
on the tent

above
me

Someone

painted a smile
on
the sun

the
graffiti
of a clown

in
a

hurry.

WATCHING

shadows
walk
beside you

means the sun
is

out.

You can't ride an elephant every day!

OVER

the top
the ferris wheel
swung

like a magic
floating
lady

hung
in mid-air

before
the trick

was
finished.

A "prize
every time"
flirted
the hanky-pank

and
I won
a paper fan.

THE
carnival lights
punctuated
the evening sky
with
exclamation
points.

CRAZY
house
mirrors

are not for
people
who believe
what

they
see.

Clowns

putting on
a silly
nose

are what
they
want to be

becoming real
like

you & me.

THERE are worse things than a **PIE!** in the face.

PLOP

The Lion's ROAR

made
our jumping pulse

forget
the bars of time

between
wildness

&

ourselves.

Showgirls

stand
on the ground
as
if
brought to earth
to

escape.

Barely

moving inside the
ring
the bareback horse
juggled
riders from its

back
never
missing the

ground.

Youth

spins
too
quickly
through the air
for
anyone
to

catch.

Above

us
fireworks

sprout
flowers...

a
magic
garden
planted

in the sky.

FIREFLIES

light the night
circus

with
audience
underfoot
clapping 6 legs
for
all that is
small.

clap
clap clap
clap
clap
clap

The circus ends too quickly. If only I could whistle LOUDLY!

TENTS

appearing
in the morning
vanish
in the night

a trick of muscle
by
the silent man
traveling
with his past

unknown
even
to
him.

THE

circus train
stretched
slooowly
from the city
softly
saying

good-bye.

Sleep
little one
&
dream
of the ring
that
will
be
yours
tomorrow.